High in the mountains, Snowy and her family lived in a small cave.

Snowy liked to jump and play in the deep, soft snow.

Winter was almost over, and each day was a little brighter and warmer. Mama took Snowy exploring all over the mountain. One morning, they studied the tracks of other animals.

All of a sudden, there were loud, sharp sounds: bang, bang! Snowy wondered, *Is it thunder? Or an avalanche?* Then they heard human voices shouting. Snowy and her mom were afraid. "Fur hunters!" whispered Mama. Snowy knew they made many animals disappear.

"Run, Snowy!" Mama yelled.
"Hide in the forest!"

Mama ran away from her
daughter so the hunters
would follow her instead
of Snowy.

Afraid of the hunters, Snowy ran through the forest until the sky was dark.

Then she realized that she had gone too far
and was lost. Would Mama be able to find her?

Snowy curled up beside a tree and waited for
morning to come.

The next morning, feeling sad and lonely,
Snowy sat by a big tree. Suddenly, she
could hear someone breathing nearby . . .

. . . and then a clumsy little animal walked right in front of her. A marmot had just awoken from hibernating through the winter. He was busily looking for nuts and berries to eat.

Snowy and Marmot stayed together all day in the forest, hoping Snowy's mother would come. As night fell, Marmot said, "It's cold out here!"

"The cold isn't my biggest problem," Snowy answered. "I'm lost and I don't think Mama will be able to find me."

"Oh my, how sad," Marmot sighed. "I have many animal friends. Maybe we can help you find your way home."

Snowy smiled a little. "That is so nice of you, Marmot. Tonight you have one more friend. You can sleep here next to me; my fur will keep you warm."

At dawn, the darkness was fading from the forest. Owl was getting
ready to sleep when the two friends arrived under her tree.
"Good morning, Owl!" said Marmot. "Excuse us, but do you know the
way to my friend Snowy's home?"

"I am too old to remember," Owl answered in a deep voice. "From the South Peak of the mountain you can see far away and find the right path. It is very hard to get to the peak, so you need to be patient and brave. Ask help from the deer, rabbits, and sheep."

The South Peak was too far away for two little animals to walk alone. They needed Musk Deer to help them cross the wide plain.

Following Musk Deer's unusual scent, Snowy and Marmot tracked him.

Musk Deer kindly took them on his back and walked a long way. When they arrived at the mountain, Musk Deer wished them good luck and turned back.

The mountainside was steep and full of rocks.
Snowy and Marmot slowly started to climb.
Snowy was small, though, and not very good at
jumping over the rocks.

Rabbit noticed their trouble and hopped over to them. A great jumper himself, Rabbit happily gave Snowy some jumping lessons. There was no time to waste to reach the peak and look for Snowy's way home.

After a few hours of training, Snowy was able to jump over little boulders and crevices, even with Marmot on her back. Rabbit waved goodbye and hopped away.

Snowy and Marmot finally reached the last part of their journey—climbing to the peak. There were many little paths heading uphill, but they all looked too dangerous. Who could help them climb?

Marmot disappeared for a minute
and returned with a young Argali, a
mountain sheep. There was no peak
that Argali could not reach. She
agreed to lead them.

It was late afternoon when Snowy and her friends finally reached the South Peak. The view was amazing all around them. They could see far, far away.

They looked around everywhere. Snowy suddenly shouted with joy. "I can see the slope where my home is! If we follow this ridge, I think we can reach it before nighttime."

Snowy and Marmot thanked Argali and said goodbye, then walked along the ridge.

The sun was starting to set as Snowy and Marmot quickly walked. Argali had taught them to step with courage and purpose. The world around them looked so beautiful.

The two friends came
to the snowy hillside
above Snowy's
home. Their hearts
were pounding with
excitement. They ran
down the hill as fast as
they could.

It was nearly dark when they saw Snowy's mother!

"Snowy!"
"Mama! Papa!"
Mama kissed Snowy's nose, and Papa
rubbed her head. They were so happy to
be together again.

Snowy explained, "My new friend Marmot and many other forest animals taught me all that I needed to know to find my way home: kindness, patience, loyalty, and courage."

When Snowy and Mama turned to look at Marmot, he was already asleep. They'd had such a big adventure on his first day awake after winter hibernation. He needed a little rest!

The snow leopard, symbolic animal of the Himalayas, is threatened by the destruction of its natural habitat and by poaching. Learn how you can help snow leopards survive and thrive by visiting online resources such as *www.snowleopard.org* or *www.snowleopardconservancy.org*.

Happy Fox Books is an imprint of
Fox Chapel Publishing Company, Inc.,
903 Square Street, Mount Joy, PA 17552.

© 2018 Snake SA, Chemin du Tsan du Péri 10, 3971 Chermignon, Switzerland

Snowy: A Leopard of the High Mountains is an original work, first published in North America in 2018 by Fox Chapel Publishing Company, Inc. Reproduction of its contents is strictly prohibited without written permission from the rights holder.

ISBN 978-1-64124-015-4

Library of Congress Cataloging-in-Publication Data

Names: Petkovic, Milisava, author. | Xuan, Xuan Loc, illustrator.
Title: Snowy : a leopard of the high mountains / text by Milisava Petkovic ;
   illustrations by Xuan Loc Xuan.
Other titles: Nevoso il leopardo delle alte vette. English
Description: Mount Joy : Happy Fox Books, 2018. | Summary: "A snow leopard is
   lost and needs to find her mother. She overcomes danger by making new
   forest friends and learning about courage and patience"-- Provided by
   publisher. Includes facts about snow leopards and threats to their
   survival.
Identifiers: LCCN 2018012870 | ISBN 9781641240154 (hardcover)
Subjects: | CYAC: Snow leopard--Fiction. | Leopard--Fiction. | Forest
   animals--Fiction. | Animals--Infancy--Fiction. | Himalaya
   Mountains--Fiction.
Classification: LCC PZ7.1.P465 Sno 2018 | DDC [E]--dc23
LC record available at https://lccn.loc.gov/2018012870

To learn more about the other great books from
Fox Chapel Publishing, or to find a retailer near you, call toll-free
800-457-9112 or visit us at *www.FoxChapelPublishing.com*.

We are always looking for talented authors. To submit an idea, please
send a brief inquiry to acquisitions@foxchapelpublishing.com.

Fox Chapel Publishing makes every effort to use environmentally friendly paper for printing.

Printed in China

First printing

MILISAVA PETKOVIĆ

Milisava, an academic researcher, was born in the former Yugoslavia. Eager to explore the world, she spent years traveling in many countries before returning to her native land. Milisava currently works as co-editor for the Belgrade International Theatre Festival in Serbia, part of an internationally acclaimed theater festival for children and young audiences.

XUAN LOC XUAN

Born in a village in Vietnam, she studied graphic design at the prestigious Ho Chi Minh City University of Fine Arts. In her art she shows themes related to nature, using a light and delicate touch. She is a freelance illustrator living in Ho Chi Minh City, Vietnam.

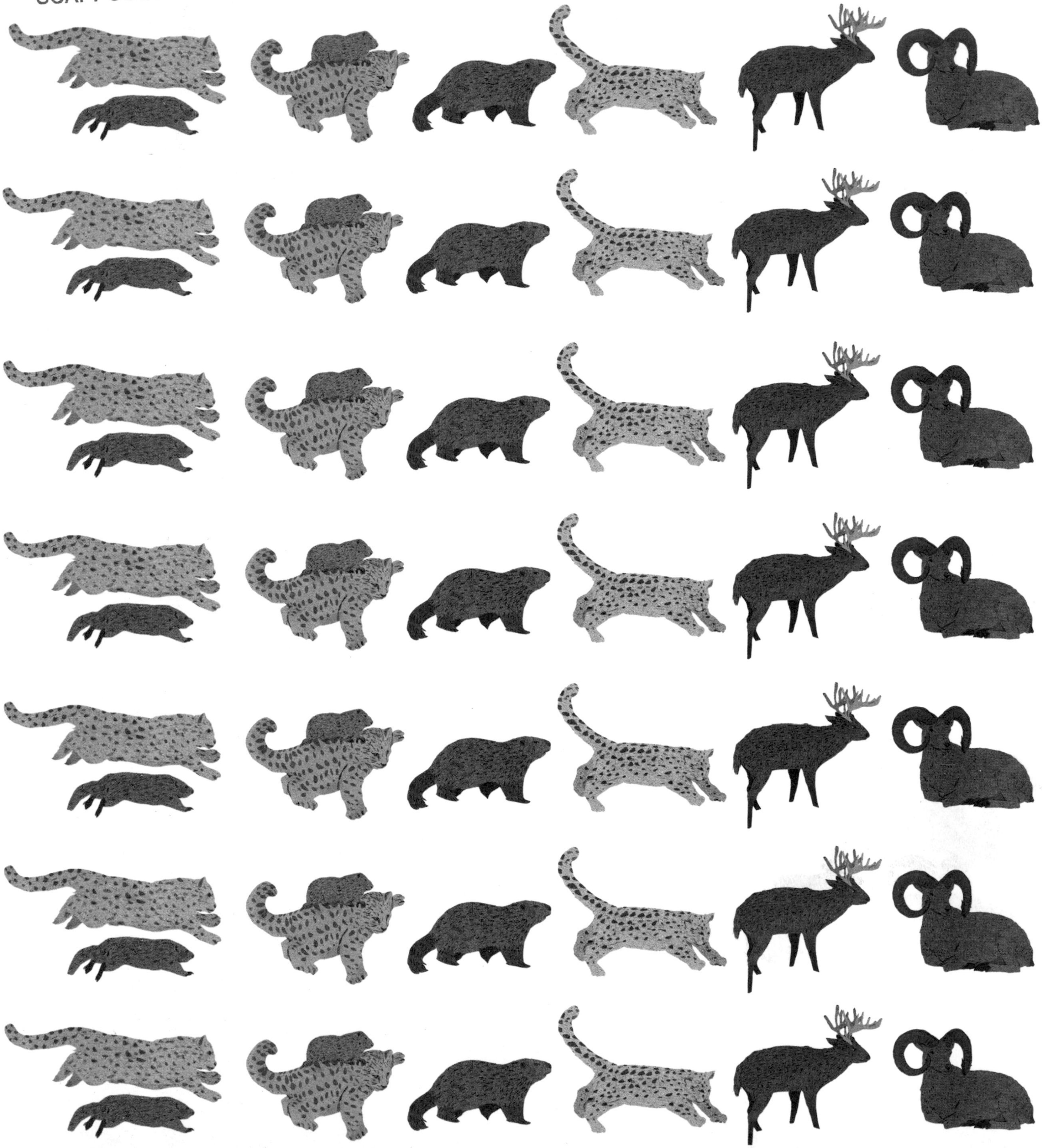

MILISAVA PETKOVIĆ

Milisava, an academic researcher, was born in the former Yugoslavia. Eager to explore the world, she spent years traveling in many countries before returning to her native land. Milisava currently works as co-editor for the Belgrade International Theatre Festival in Serbia, part of an internationally acclaimed theater festival for children and young audiences.

XUAN LOC XUAN

Born in a village in Vietnam, she studied graphic design at the prestigious Ho Chi Minh City University of Fine Arts. In her art she shows themes related to nature, using a light and delicate touch. She is a freelance illustrator living in Ho Chi Minh City, Vietnam.